Monsters a[...]

Written by Heather Gemmen

Illustrated by Luciano Lagares

Based on *A Sombra do Medo* by: Célia Ghueire

www.cookcommunications.com/kidz

Faith Parenting Guide

Ages 4-7

Grace

A Faith Parenting Guide can be found at the back of book.

I know some kids who feel afraid
Each time they go to bed.

As if a monster with big teeth
Would bite them on the head.

As if a monster with sharp claws
Would growl, "I'll get you!"
If there really was such thing
Then I would worry, too.

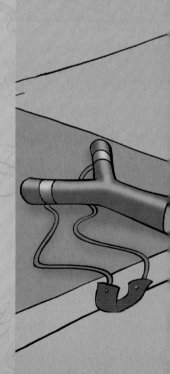

I'd worry big; I'd worry loud.
I'd worry all night long.
'Cause catching kids with swords and claws
Is scary—and it's wrong.

My grandpa says there's no such thing—
And I believe he's right.
But then I sometimes wonder why
I see strange things at night.

If there was this scary thing—
Whose tongue was long and red,
Who had sharp spikes and great big feet—
I'd hide beneath my spread.

And if it came to snatch me up
And stuff me in its sack,
I'd twist and struggle, scream and fight,
And bump against its back.

13

No! That isn't what I'd do!
I'd do what David did!
I'd pray to God and beat this lug
Although I'm just a kid.

It doesn't matter who I am—
I could be big or small.
God will help me every time.
I just have to call.

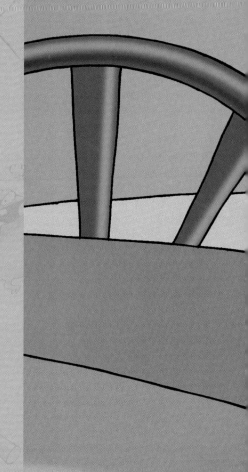

I'd grab my spread right off the bed
Without a hint of fear.
I'd look the creature in the eye
And watch him coming near.

The monster soon would hesitate
And start to back away.
Then I would run to grab more stuff—
And pray and pray and pray!

20

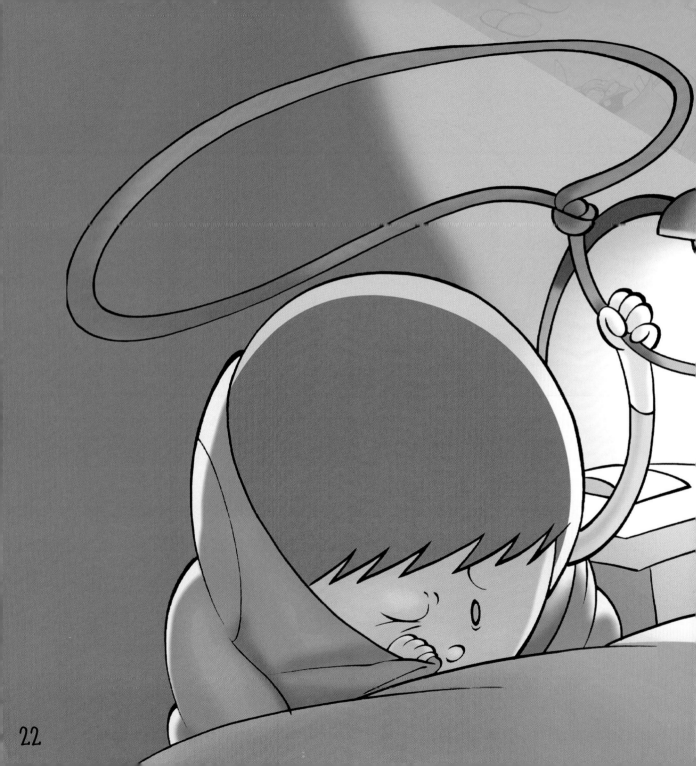

I'd kneel right down beside my bed,
Take very careful aim,
Swing my lasso overhead,
And put this creep to shame.

23

As I thought these lofty thoughts
My grandpa wandered in.
"I thought that you would want your toys
Stored safely in your bin."

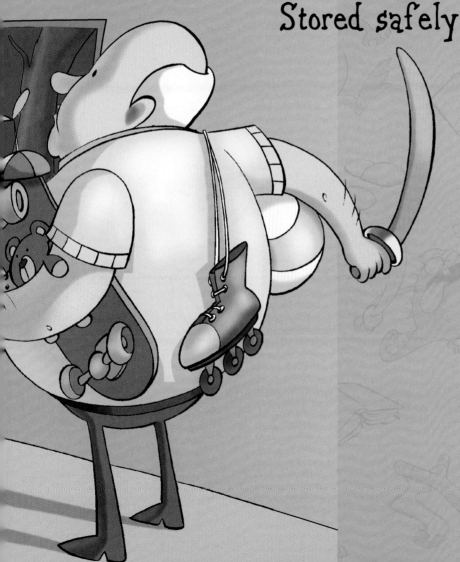

I asked my grandpa lots of things
'Bout scary monster guys.
I told him how it works to pray—
And Grandpa said I'm wise.

I think I know how David felt
When he was just a boy.
He trusted God and then he squashed
Goliath like a toy.

My grandpa's smart and I will tell
All the things he said
To all the kids who feel afraid
Each time they go to bed.

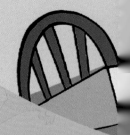

Monsters at Night

Life Issue: I want my children to feel secure in God's care.

Spiritual Building Block: Peace

Help your children to trust God in the following ways:

Sight: Let your children stay up late one night so that your entire family can lie on the grass and watch the stars. Help your children to grasp how huge the universe God created is. Tell them that this mighty God is the very One who cares for each of them.

Sound: Your children may often hear formal prayer at church and around the dinner table, but they may not so often hear a personal word of thanksgiving to God for his constant presence in our lives. On occasion, let your children in on your personal prayers so they can begin to feel comfortable speaking to this King who is also their Father.

Touch: Earthly parents—imperfect though we are—represent God's perfect care to our children. By being with your kids in times of fear and listening to their concerns, you are helping them to learn what it means to rest in God's love. Next time your children express fear, praise them for voicing their feelings and then stay with them and pray with them until they feel secure again.